toenail SOUP

by C.M. Walsh

First Printing, 2018
ISBN 978-1-7326169-1-2
Thirteen Stories Publishing
36500 Ford Road #156
Westland, MI 48185
thirteenstoriespublishing.com

Cover Design/Illustration by John Rose

Thank you, John Rose, for sharing your talent and creating such an awesome book cover.

Mike Connor, tons of thanks. You and your staff are amazing, and I am deeply grateful for your illustrative flair. Don't worry, your toenail story is safe with me.

To my sister, without you, this book would not be possible. Thank you from the bottom of my heart.

To my children, thank you for allowing your song from twenty years ago to once again take life.

To my husband, thank you for your love and support.

Toenail Soup

Contents

Chapter 1

The Not So Ordinary Joey Martin

For the most part, second grader, Joey Martin is an ordinary seven-year-old boy. He enjoys watching bugs crawl around the yard and playing fetch with his dog, Bo.

Joey also giggles when he hears the word FART, and sometimes he picks his nose.

There is ONE thing that makes Joey different from all of his friends; he loves when his mom

cooks up his

favorite dinner,

toenail soup!

Where does toenail soup come from?

The refrigerator of course, and Joey's imagination.

You see, even though he is only seven, Joey's mom would have him come up with ideas for dinner.

Not too long ago, while Joey was playing in his backyard, his mom hollered out the window, "Joey, would you like to help me with dinner tonight?"

"Sure."

As he entered the kitchen, Joey noticed a big pot waited on the stove for the ingredients.

"What should we include?"

"Hmmm." Joey mouthed as he went through the refrigerator grabbing all the food he could.

After looking at everything Joey had placed on the counter, his mom giggled to herself and then asked, "are you sure?"

"Yep."

"Okay." His mother grinned as she started mixing everything in the pot. Joey headed back outside while his mom cooked dinner.

It wasn't long before Joey heard, "come and eat."

As he sat down at the table, Joey couldn't help but smell what was coming. He was hungry.

"It smells delicious!"

Joey's mom placed a bowl of soup before him and wrinkled her nose.

"If you say so."

Chapter 2

Floating Green Globs

The first time he looked down at his soup,

Joey saw floating green globs that

reminded him of the gunk that gathered

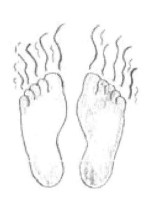

under his toenails

after a long day of

playing outside. Boy,

did it stink! It stunk

like feet! After a few

big whiffs of the smelly creation, Joey decided to call it toenail soup.

The soup smelled so terrible Joey's mom had to open the kitchen window whenever the soup was cooking. She would exclaim, "it smells like your stinky feet after you play a game of baseball!" Which made Joey smile ear to ear.

As he bit into brussels sprouts and bacon bits that peeked out from the hot soup, Joey thought they crunched like freshly cut toenail nuggets.

CRUNCH, CRUNCH, CRUNCH.

"How's the soup tonight Joey?" his mom asked every time she made it. Without looking up from his bowl, he would reply, "yum!"

To Joey, it was delicious, to everyone else, it was gross.

Chapter 3

Joey's Song

Joey loved his toenail soup so much he even wrote a song about it!

Toenail Soup

(Sung to the tune: On Top of Spaghetti)

One day I was hungry,

and had nothing to eat,

so I clipped all my toenails,

and made a wonderful treat.

It looks good in the ladle,

I can eat the whole pot,

if I hurry and guzzle,

but I'd rather not.

With lots of chunks floating,

my mother will cook,

the world's best toenail soup,

loaded with gobbledygook.

So, don't eat my treat,

unless you like things,

that are certainly smelly,

plus yellow and green.

Chapter 4

Stinky and Weird

On a Friday afternoon, while his mother cooked toenail soup in the kitchen, Joey played outside with his best friends, Mike Hanson and Gabe Dayley.

In a matter of minutes, the smell of the soup filled their nostrils.

Wow, what's that smell?" inquired Gabe as he adjusted his cap.

Mike quickly asked, "is that your supper, Joey?"

"It's toenail soup, and yep, it's for supper."

They both made faces as Gabe replied, "sorry for you, that stuff stinks!"

As they packed up their baseball gear and started to head home, Gabe turned around and uttered, "you are so...weird."

Saddened, Joey hung his head and ran inside to eat. As he looked at his soup, Joey knew he wasn't weird, and if his friends would only try it, they may like the soup as much as he did.

As usual, Joey ate every last drop and thanked his

mom.

Chapter 5

Toey Joey

When Joey arrived at school Monday morning the kids playing outside laughed at him as he walked by. Then it began, a chant,

"Toey Joey,"

"Toey Joey,"

"Toey Joey."

Before Joey could say anything, most of the kids were calling him "Toey Joey."

As he bolted into the school building,

Joey wiped away the tears that ran down

his face.

He couldn't believe it; his best friends had

told everyone about his soup and how

awful they thought it was.

How would they know, they hadn't even tasted it, and now everyone was making fun of him.

Joey knew right then it was going to be a bad day. And, it was.

That night he didn't say anything to his mom about what happened at school. Joey thought tomorrow would be different. All of his classmates would be nice, and everything would be back to normal.

Chapter 6

A Bad Week

Sadly, Tuesday at school was worse. "Toey Joey" was chanted by all the kids, including some Joey didn't know.

Even though he hated being teased and wanted to disappear, Joey understood that wouldn't make anything better. No, running away wasn't the answer. He just had to show everyone he wasn't weird.

After an entire week of the kids teasing him, Joey finally told his mom what was going on. "I noticed something was bothering you."

She kissed Joey's forehead, and whispered, "everything will be okay, it will all work out." Nodding to his mom, Joey realized she was right and spent the weekend figuring out ways to stop the kids from teasing him.

Monday came, and Joey felt it was going to be a good day, somehow. As he entered the school, Joey noticed a poster on the wall by the office; it was the answer! It would be a great day!

Chapter 7

Joey's Answer

FLAVOR FESTIVAL

SHARE YOUR FAVORITE KITCHEN CREATIONS

WHEN: THIS SATURDAY AT NOON

WHERE: LARGE GYM

SIGN UP: TODAY THROUGH FRIDAY IN THE OFFICE

TABLES WILL BE PROVIDED. YOU CAN DECORATE
THEM. YOU CAN EVEN SET UP A DISPLAY WITH
INFORMATION ABOUT YOUR FAVORITE FOOD.

EVERYONE IS INVITED!

Joey immediately opened the office door and asked for the signup sheet. As he looked at it, he noticed twenty-five kids had already signed up. Perfect, Joey thought to himself. There would be plenty of people at the festival to try the soup.

Excitedly, he scribbled down his information and handed the list back to the secretary, who glanced down and muttered, "toenail soup?"

"Yep,"

Joey walked to class, once again smiling ear to ear.

He knew things were about to change.

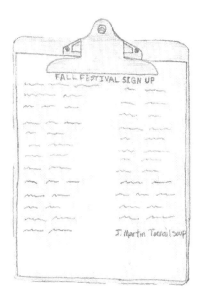

Chapter 8

Getting Ready

That whole week Joey heard the chant "Toey Joey," except this time he ignored the name calling and went about planning for the Flavor Festival.

Every night Joey worked on the display that would sit on his festival table. He wrote the words to his toenail soup song on the board with bright markers, so it was easy to read.

Joey's mom spent the week chopping enough brussels sprouts and other ingredients to cook plenty of soup for anyone who wanted a taste.

Saturday came, and the smell of toenail soup blew through the house.

Joey couldn't help but smile as he sang his song all morning until it was time to head up to the school.

As excited as Joey was, his stomach hurt a bit because he was nervous the kids would tease him again.

Before he knew it, they had arrived at the school and all Joey could do was stare at the building.

There it was; the school entrance, wide open with a huge sign that read, "Flavor

Festival Today."

Joey took a deep breath and grabbed his display. His mom clutched the pot of soup, and in they went.

Chapter 9

Flavor Festival

In the gym, people scurried about setting up their tables and tasted food that was ready for sharing. Joey arranged his table and eagerly waited for someone to try his soup.

For the first hour, no one came over to Joey's table. He sat there feeling worse than when he walked in.

So what if others thought his soup smelled awful. Joey believed if they tasted it they would like it as much as he did.

After he looked around the gym a few times, Joey realized there were so many people to share his soup with.

This was his only chance, he had to do something, he had nothing to lose.

Joey quickly grabbed the microphone

that was resting on a stand next to his table and walked up onto the stage built for the festival's announcers.

No one noticed him, until...

Joey cleared his throat and sang his toenail soup song loud enough everyone could hear.

Heads started turning toward Joey and people began to approach his table. Some made faces as the smell swirled around the group. A hand raised in the crowd, then a voice, "I would like to try your soup." It was the principal!

As he grabbed his sample of toenail soup, the principal commented, "it smells very interesting Joey."

SLURP. CRUNCH.

The principal looked at Joey and smiled. "This soup is delicious!"

Before long, several grownups were slurping and crunching throughout the gym.

As good as that made Joey feel, none of the kids had tasted the soup.

CRUNCH

SLURP

Chapter 10

Slurp, Crunch

There they were, Mike and Gabe who started the whole "Toey Joey" name calling. They were the reason all of Joey's classmates had made fun of him for the last two weeks.

They stood at Joey's table staring at the soup.

"I dare you to try it Gabe," Mike urged.

"Nah, I'm good. That stuff smells awful."

"Chicken." Mike teased as he grabbed a bowl.

Raising the spoon up to his mouth in slow motion, Mike winced, "here goes nothing." In a flash, the soup was gone. Mike turned around and asked if he could have another sample.

"This stuff is really good Joey," Mike admitted between slurps and crunches

Gabe was shocked. He couldn't think of anything to say so he just stood there with his mouth wide open.

That was it. He had to try the soup out.

After a few bites, Gabe quickly agreed with Mike and asked for a second helping.

One by one the children made their way to taste Joey's creation, and one by one they slurped and crunched in delight.

Soon the pot of soup was empty, every bite eaten up before the festival was over. Joey's stomach stopped hurting, and he smiled. Until Monday...

Chapter 11

Back to School

As Joey's mom drove him to the school, Joey's mind was flooded with thoughts, would the kids be mean to him again? Had they been polite because their parents were with them at the festival? Would they continue to call him names?

Joey hoped the answer to all of his questions was no, but the only way to find out was to get out of the car.

"Have a great day Joey."

"Thanks mom, you too."

Still nervous, Joey headed off to the playground, where he could hear his toenail soup song coming from a group of kids.

He thought, uh-oh, were they about to tease him again? Joey didn't have to wonder any longer.

He was quickly surrounded by all of the schoolkids, including Mike and Gabe, who put their arms around Joey and patted him on the back.

"That soup was amazing!" exclaimed Mike.

Gabe added, "I agree."

"I loved it," said one kid.

"Me too," yelled out another from the back of the group.

They all admitted they were wrong for teasing Joey about his soup and they thought it was pretty cool he created something yucky, yet, so yummy.

Once all the apologies and pats on the back were over, they all ran around and danced to Joey's toenail soup song.

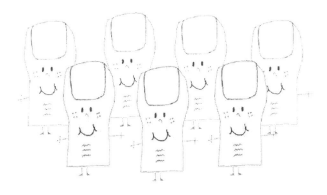

They all had become "Toey Joeys."

His friends and classmates had come to realize they were much more like Joey than different.

And to that, Joey smiled.

Chapter 12

Toenail Soup Recipe

½ lb. Bacon (fried and crumbled)

3 cups Pasta (cooked and drained)*

1 lb. Fresh Brussels Sprouts or frozen
(thaw before using)

½ lb. Petite Medley or Fingerling
Potatoes cubed (Joey leaves the
skins on)

1 med. Onion diced

2 Tb. Butter

4 cups Chicken Broth

10.5 oz. can Cream of Mushroom Soup

1/2 cup Heavy Cream

1 Egg Yolk

Chopped Parsley (fresh or dried)

Salt and Pepper to taste

In a large saucepan melt butter and sauté the onion and cubed potatoes until onion is tender. Add the brussels sprouts and chicken broth, bring to a boil. Cover and simmer for 10-15 minutes or until vegetables are tender.

Mix egg yolk and cream in small bowl and pour a small amount of the hot soup slowly into the mixture while stirring constantly. Once combined, pour the egg mixture back into the saucepan. Stir.

Add the can of cream of mushroom soup and simmer an additional 2-3 minutes. Do not boil after adding the egg yolk mixture. (boiling will "scramble" the egg yolk)

Add pasta and heat through.

Garnish with crumbled bacon and chopped parsley.

Salt and pepper soup to taste.

*Joey used leftover spaghetti.

48

Thank you for reading my book. If you enjoyed it, won't you please take a moment to leave me a review at your favorite retailer.

Thanks!
C. M. Walsh

About the Author

C. M. Walsh is the mother of five children. She grew up in the Midwest and holds undergraduate degrees in Psychology and Sociology. C. M. also earned a culinary degree in 2007. She lives in Michigan with her husband, youngest child and her dog, Annie.

Connect with Me

Twitter: twitter.com/onewittywriter
Facebook: facebook.com/writeallday
Blog: https://thewittywriter.com

Made in the USA
Monee, IL
21 September 2020